Rohu
Long-Teeth

For Pim and
Morgan, with love
— F. P.

To my beloved
nieces, Zoe and
Gala — S. F.

Barefoot Books
2067 Massachusetts Ave
Cambridge, MA 02140

First published in the United States of America by Barefoot Books, Inc in 2013
This story is an abridged version of a chapter of
The Barefoot Book of Monsters, published in 2003

Graphic design by Judy Linard, London, UK
Reproduction by B & P International, Hong Kong
Printed in China on 100% acid-free paper
This book was typeset in Chalkduster, Gilligan's Island and Sassoon Primary
The illustrations were prepared in acrylics

Thank you to the pupils of Cutteslowe Primary School, Oxford, UK
for all their careful reading.

Sources:
Alpers, Anthony. *Legends of the South Seas*. John Murray Ltd, London, 1970.

Mackenzie, D.A. *Myths and Traditions of the South Sea Islands*.
Gresham Publishing Co. Ltd, London, 1930.

ISBN 978-1-84686-908-2

Library of Congress Cataloging-in-Publication Data
is available under LCCN 2012037069

1 3 5 7 9 8 6 4 2

Rona Long-Teeth

A Story from Tahiti

Retold by Fran Parnell • Illustrated by Sophie Fatus

Barefoot Books

step inside a story

Contents

CHAPTER 1

The Monster's Daughter

On the island of Tahiti, there once lived an evil she-monster. Her name was Rona Long-Teeth. She knew many powerful spells, and her heart was dark and evil.

Rona Long-Teeth's home was a
little hut in a clearing among the
banana trees. She lived there with
her baby daughter, Hina. Now, Hina
was kind and good. She was always
smiling and singing and always helpful
to everyone she met. And she did not
know that her mother was a monster.

Rona Long-Teeth loved her daughter dearly. Every day, she would rub the little girl's skin with sandalwood oil to make it soft and sweet. Every day, she would comb Hina's long, dark hair until it shone like water.

Every day, she would
smooth the tips of Hina's
fingers until they were more
slender and delicate than any
fingers you have ever seen.

Thank you,
Mom.

Rona Long-Teeth fed Hina with the best mangoes and pineapples so that her daughter would grow up strong and healthy.

She caught the fattest crabs on the reef, and cooked their sweet meat for her daughter.

As the years passed, the monster's child grew up. She was a beautiful young woman.

But even though she loved Hina, Rona Long-Teeth felt nothing for the people on the island.

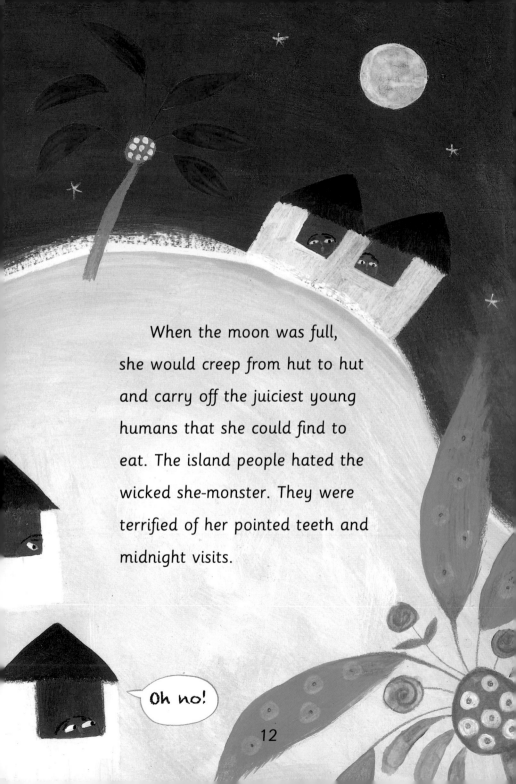

When the moon was full,
she would creep from hut to hut
and carry off the juiciest young
humans that she could find to
eat. The island people hated the
wicked she-monster. They were
terrified of her pointed teeth and
midnight visits.

Oh no!

Hina knew nothing of her
mother's evil ways. If ever she woke
in the night and found her mother
was gone, she simply thought that
Rona Long-Teeth had gone fishing
for crabs in the moonlight.

13

CHAPTER 2

The Secret Cave

I can't stay here.

On the same island, there lived a young man whose name was Monoi. One night, Monoi decided that he could not bear to live in fear of Rona Long-Teeth any longer. He ran to a special place he knew, where there was a high cliff beside a pool with palm trees growing all around it. There was a cave in the cliff, and Monoi hid there.

He laid bark mats down to
make the cave floor soft and dry. Then
he sang a special charm-song, which
helped him roll a big rock in front of
the cave so that no one could see it
from the outside. When he wanted
to leave the cave to find food or
breathe the clear morning air,
he would sing the charm-song
again and the rock would open.

15

It so happened that the pool with the palm trees all around was Hina's favorite place to swim. One day, Monoi saw her swimming in the pool. He fell head over heels in love with her. He forgot his fear and climbed down the cliff to talk to her.

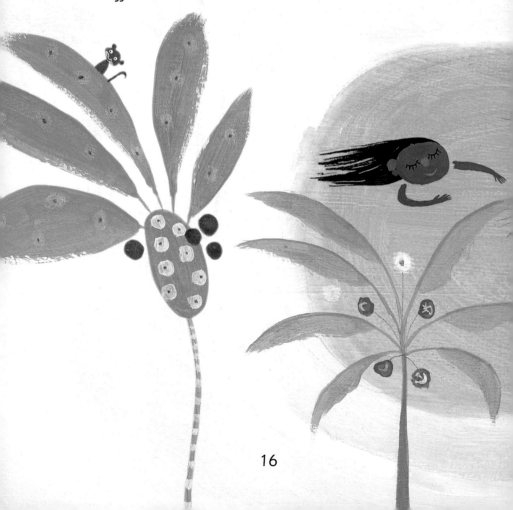

Monoi was kind and handsome.
Hina fell in love with him at once. They
sat by the pool, singing songs and telling
jokes. But Monoi would not tell Hina
where he lived.

"I know your mother is Rona Long-
Teeth," Monoi said. "If she knows where
I am, she might come and eat me!"

I love
you.

17

Hina had no idea that Rona Long-Teeth ate human beings. She was very upset. She promised she would never tell her mother where Monoi lived. So Monoi showed her his secret cave and told her he would always come out if she stood outside and called to him.

I'll come back tomorrow.

CHAPTER 3

The
PiCNiC

The very next day, as soon as Rona
Long-Teeth had gone out to fish for their
supper, Hina packed a basket full of food.
Then she ran down to the bottom of the
high cliff and sang:

"Here is your friend!

Come out and have fun.

Push open the rock,

And we'll dance in the sun!"

From inside the cave, Monoi answered:

"Where is your mother,

    With her teeth sharp and long?

Answer me that,

    And I'll sing the charm-song."

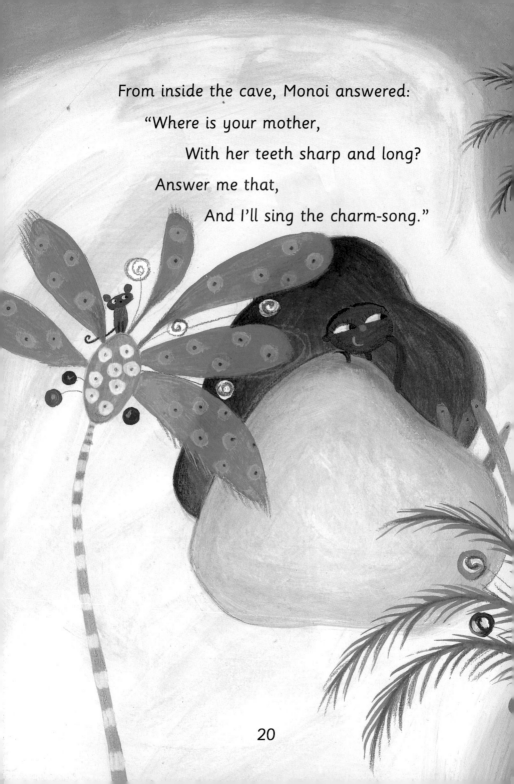

"She's on the long reef;
    She's on the short reef.
She's catching crabs
    For the two of us to eat!" sang Hina.

21

Then Monoi sang the charm-song,
and came hurrying out of the cave.

The two of them played together all
morning, and when the sun was high in
the sky, they sat by the water and ate
the picnic that Hina had brought.

"My heart belongs to you," Monoi said
to Hina. "I'll love you forever."

Then, as the sun started to sink lower in the sky, he climbed back into his hiding place. Hina hurried away. She got home just before Rona Long-Teeth came back with a basket full of crabs.

But Rona was clever. She noticed how much food was missing from the hut.

"Where has all our food gone?" she muttered to herself. "Hina has eaten like a little pig today! Something odd is going on here, and I shall find out what it is."

The very next morning, the crafty monster hugged her belly and moaned softly. Then she lay down.

"I don't feel well," she groaned. "I think I will stay here and sleep until I feel better. My poor old legs are too weak to walk to the reef today." She lay still and then began to snore.

Hina wanted to see Monoi again very
badly. As soon as she heard her mother
begin to snore, she packed a picnic basket
and ran to the cliff.

I must see
Monoi again.

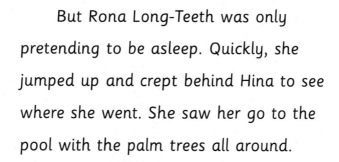

But Rona Long-Teeth was only pretending to be asleep. Quickly, she jumped up and crept behind Hina to see where she went. She saw her go to the pool with the palm trees all around.

She watched Hina singing and
Monoi jumping out from the cave.
Rona Long-Teeth was furious. Her
blood boiled, and she ground
her teeth in rage.

"Young he looks, and
tasty too," she snarled to
herself. "I shall eat him up
by and by."

CHAPTER 4

A MidNight FeaSt

That night, Rona said to her daughter, "Hina dear, I'm feeling much better tonight. I think I will go fishing by torchlight, and when I get back we can have an early breakfast of breadfruit, yams and some delicious fresh fish."

"I'm so glad you're better, Mother," replied Hina with a smile. "Fresh fish for breakfast will be very nice."

Off Rona went, tiptoeing through the
dark, until she came to Monoi's cave.
She stood outside the cave and sang as
sweetly as she could:

"Here is your friend!

Come out and have fun.

Open the rock,

And we'll dance all night long!"

But Monoi was not fooled. "You are not Hina!" he shouted. "You're Rona Long-Teeth, and I'm not coming out!"

No!

Rona did not care. She was a powerful monster, and she was a magician too. She knew lots of spells. She knew a magic word that would open the cave.

"Vahia!" she screamed, and the rock cracked open with a sound like thunder. In rushed the she-monster. The teeth in her mouth grew longer and longer, and suddenly there were fangs all over her body – on her chin, on her elbows, on her knees and her back. Her whole body was covered in big, sharp teeth.

She opened her mouth wide, and before Monoi could even squeak, Rona Long-Teeth had gobbled him up, every last bit. Every last bit, that is, except for his heart.

His heart belonged to Hina. It hid
itself behind a rock.

Then Rona Long-Teeth went off to
catch fish in the reef.

Hina was fast asleep in her hut, but
when Rona Long-Teeth ate up Monoi, her
heart gave a terrible lurch. She knew that
something awful had happened. She ran
to the cliff and saw that the rock had been
broken in two.

She ran inside the cave. It was empty
and dark. Then she heard Monoi's voice
coming from a corner of the cave. It was
his heart calling out to her.

Hina ran into the cave and found the
heart. She picked it up and ran home.

CHAPTER 5

BreaKFaSt

I must be quick.

When Hina got home, Monoi's heart told her what to do. "Find the leaf of a banana tree that is as tall as you are, and cut it down," whispered the heart. "Lay it on your sleeping mat, and put a coconut where your head would be. Then cover everything up with your blanket." When Hina had done all this, it looked just as if she was still fast asleep in her bed.

"Now," said Monoi's heart, "you
must go as quickly as you can to
Chief Noa. Tell him everything that
has happened tonight, and ask him to
get his spear ready."

Hina ran across the dark island
as fast as her legs would carry her.

In the very early morning, just before dawn, Rona Long-Teeth came home with a basket full of fresh fish. She called out to Hina, but the shape in the bed did not stir.

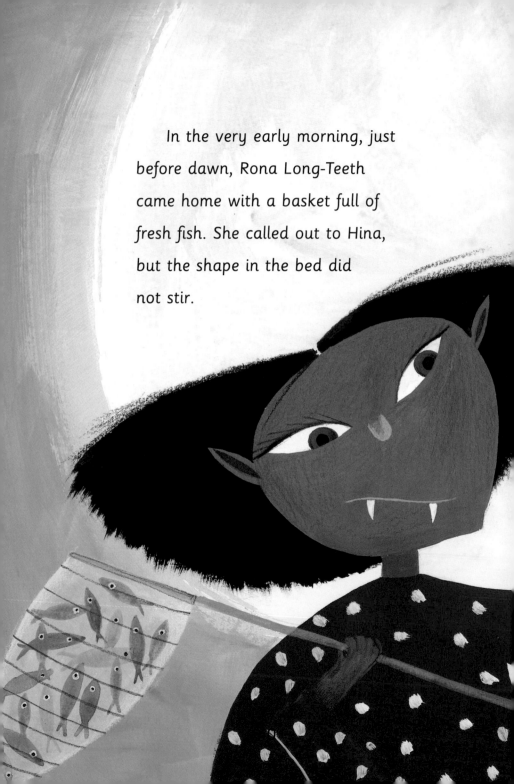

"Ah, poor child, she is tired out!" said Rona Long-Teeth. She lit a small fire. After an hour, she called, "Hina, come and sing to me while I cook our breakfast." But the shape in the bed did not stir.

"Ah, poor child, I'll let her sleep a little longer," muttered the wicked she-monster. When the fish were cooked to a crisp, Rona Long-Teeth called out, "Hina, get up, your breakfast is ready!" But still the shape in the bed did not stir.

Rona Long-Teeth went over to the bed and pulled the soft tapa cloth off the bed.

When she saw the coconut and the
banana leaf lying on Hina's sleeping
mat, she was filled with rage. She
knew she had been tricked.

It's a trick!

As the sun rose, Rona Long-Teeth
roared across the island. "Where is
Hina?" she screamed. "Where has my
daughter gone?"

The people on the island were
terrified. But they stood bravely
outside their huts and pointed to
Chief Noa's house. Rona Long-Teeth
ran in through the door.

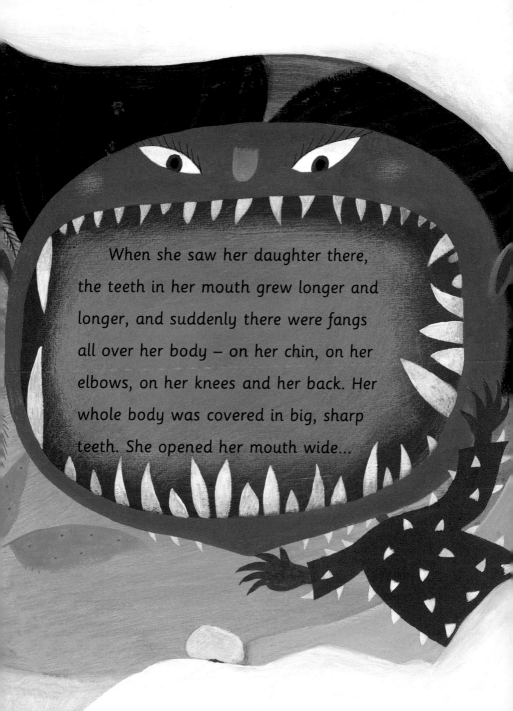

When she saw her daughter there, the teeth in her mouth grew longer and longer, and suddenly there were fangs all over her body — on her chin, on her elbows, on her knees and her back. Her whole body was covered in big, sharp teeth. She opened her mouth wide...

46

Look out!

But Chief Noa had his spear
ready, and just before Rona could
close her jaws and gobble Hina up,
the chief stuck his spear into the
she-monster and killed her.

Then Chief Noa gave Monoi's
heart to his best enchanter. The
enchanter made a new body for
Monoi and set the heart inside it.

Monoi and Hina fell into each other's arms, and the chief married them at once. And now that Rona Long-Teeth was dead and gone, everyone on the island lived in peace and harmony for the rest of their days.